W9-DHM-423

FRIENDS
OF ACPL

The Coconut Thieves

The Coconut Thieves

adapted by

CATHARINE FOURNIER

illustrated by

JANINA DOMANSKA

CHARLES SCRIBNER'S SONS
NEW YORK

Grateful acknowledgment is made to Wanda Markowska and Anna Milska for permission to translate and adapt the story of The Coconut Thieves.

A-4.64 [CLJ]
Printed in the United States
L.C.C.C. No. 64-16183

Once upon a time there was a selfish Leopard who lived in a house at the edge of a fine grove of coconut palms. The Leopard

claimed that all the coconuts in the grove were his. He swore he would tear to pieces any animal who tried to take even one.

Now the Turtle heard about the Leopard's threat, but he was not in the least impressed.

One day, when the coconuts were ripe, he paid a visit to his faithful friend the Dog. They talked about the weather and the hard times.

Suddenly the Turtle said, "Dear friend, the Leopard's coconuts are ripe. Don't you think that this would be a good time to try them?"

"I must admit," said the Dog, "that I have wanted to try them for a long time. But have you heard what the Leopard threatens to do to anyone who takes them?"

"Oh, that's silly," said the Turtle. "And of course they don't really belong to him. Don't worry. I am sure that somehow we can manage it. Let us start out tomorrow at sunrise. But could you come by my place, dear friend, and wake me? You know how hard it is for me to get up in the morning."

Early the next day the Dog, carrying a bright new cloth bag, knocked at the door of the Turtle's house.

"I am almost ready," called the Turtle in a sleepy voice. In a little while he appeared with a large bag over his arm. The two friends set out on their trip to the coconut grove.

For a time they walked along without speaking. The Turtle never liked conversation before breakfast. Finally, however, he broke the silence.

"There is something I almost forgot to tell you," the Turtle said. "Occasionally the coconuts fall from the trees. One may hit you, and that can be a little painful. Dear friend, you must promise that if this happens you will not cry out. Just grit your teeth and bear the pain in silence."

The Dog looked at his friend reproachfully. "Why, we would be lost if the Leopard should hear us," he said. "Do you really think I would be so stupid as to cry out?"

"That's very easy to say," remarked the Turtle sadly. "Actually you might save yourself by running, but with my short legs I could never get away."

"Do not be concerned, my friend. I would never even groan, much less cry out," promised the Dog.

They were still discussing the chances of a coconut falling on them when they came to the grove of stately trees. Many fine ripe

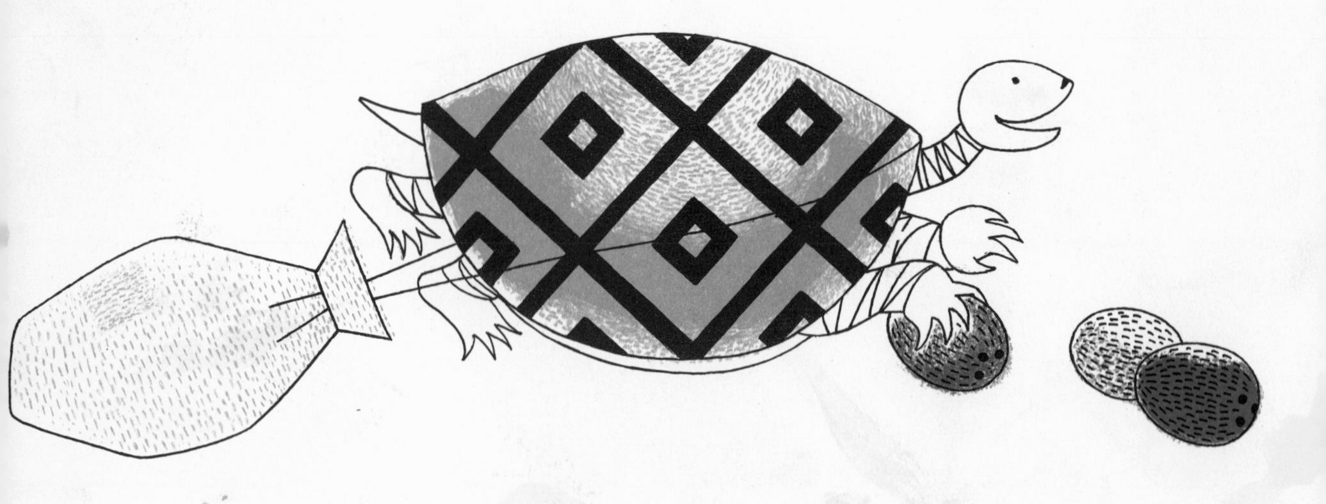

coconuts lay on the ground. The Turtle began to put them into his bag. The Dog ran about, happily wagging his tail and rolling the coconuts together, so the Turtle could pick them up more easily.

Suddenly, with a loud KNOCK, a coconut dropped on the Turtle's back. But he felt no pain through his thick shell and quietly went on with his work.

The coconuts looked so good, and the Dog was so excited at the prospect of a delicious meal, he completely forgot the Turtle's warn-

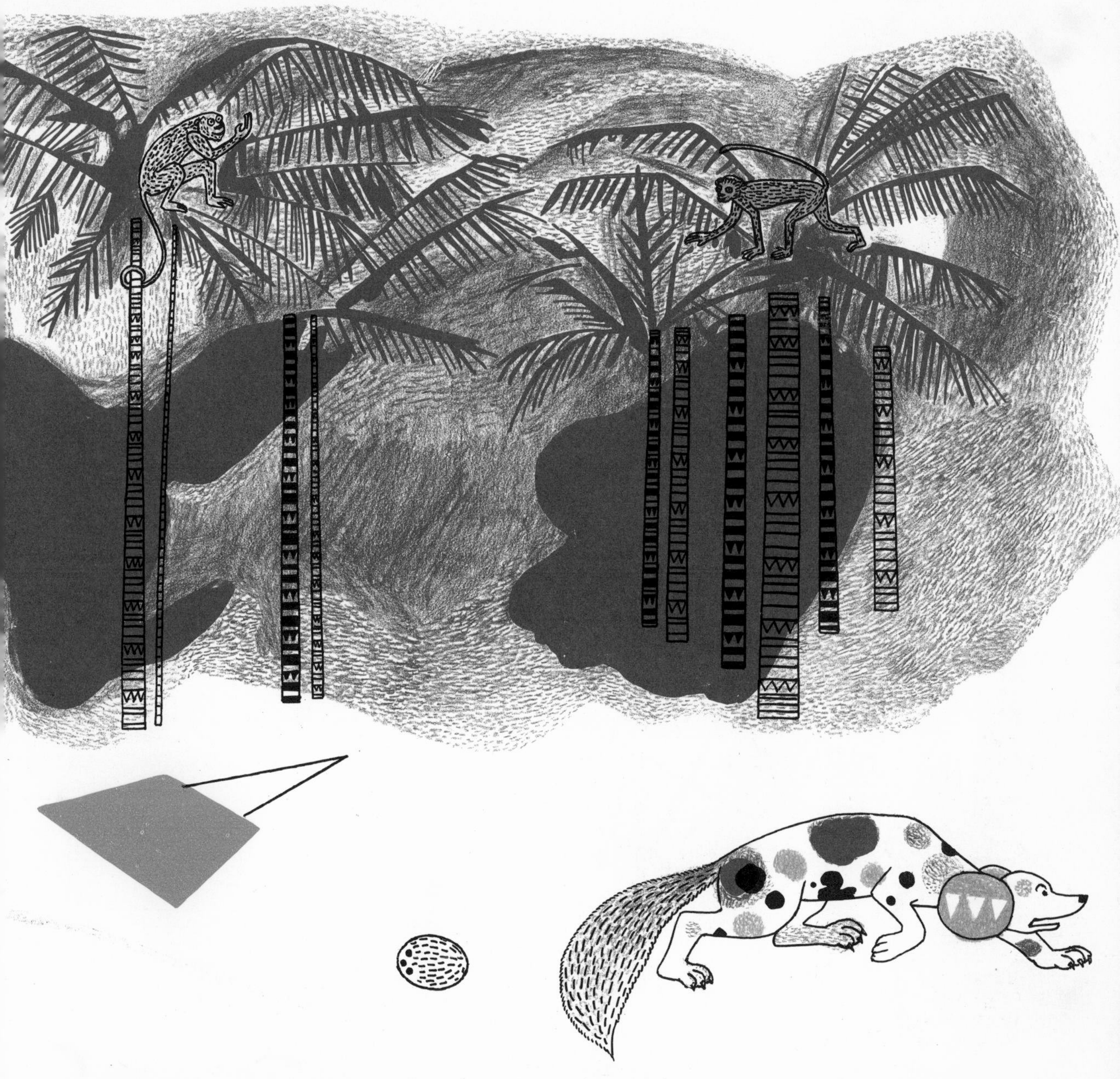

ing. It was not long before the branches rustled and again an enormous coconut fell, this time right on the Dog's head.

"Ow! Ow! Ow!" howled the Dog. He dropped his bag, put his tail between his legs, and ran away whimpering. He never gave a thought to his friend the Turtle.

"Alas! What has he done to me?" whispered the frightened Turtle. He could already hear the Leopard approaching, and he scrambled under some dry mimosa leaves just in time. Peering out, he saw the Leopard bound from the bush.

"Thief!" shrieked the enraged Leopard, as he found the Dog's bag on the ground. "I will catch you!"

The Leopard began to search for the thief. The Turtle was so afraid, a chill ran down his back. In desperation he crawled under the roots of a large tree.

But the Leopard, passing by the tree, pushed away the leaves with his paws and looked right into the Turtle's frightened eyes.

"Aha! I have you!" he cried. He held up the Dog's bag and was about to drop the Turtle into it. The Turtle, however, knew that his own bag was old and worn.

"It's too bad you have to use that new bag," the Turtle said. "I am so dirty, mine would be better."

"You are right," said the Leopard, and he put the Turtle into his own bag.

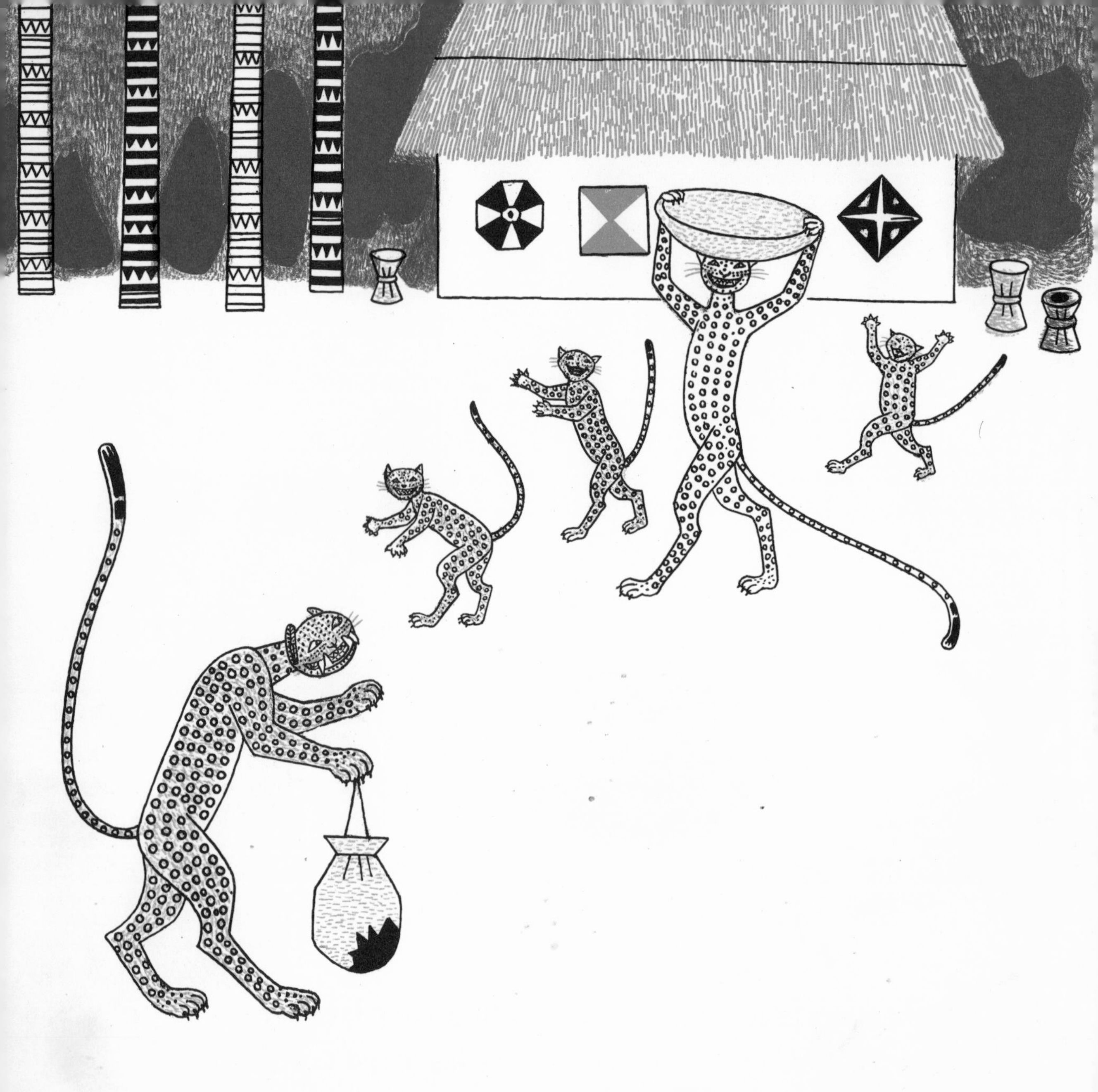

The Leopard had gone only a few steps when the Turtle began to chew on a worn place in the side of his bag. In a short time he was able to slip out through a hole he made, leaving only coconuts in the old bag.

He rested quietly in the grass until the unsuspecting Leopard was out of sight. Then he began to think of how his friend had failed him. Saddened, and a little annoyed, he set out to find the Dog.

The Leopard returned home triumphantly and immediately started to order his family about. He commanded his wife to put a pot of water on the fire, and he sent his children to invite all his friends for a feast of turtle meat.

When the animals had gathered in the house, the Leopard grandly opened the bag. To everyone's astonishment out of the bag fell, not a Turtle, but a few coconuts. At first the guests burst out laughing. They weren't too fond of the Leopard who had a

reputation for being mean and selfish. Then they thought the Leopard might be making fun of them, and they all left, growling and howling and trumpeting angrily.

The Turtle, meanwhile, had found the Dog. At great length the Dog tried to explain his behavior. Finally, he admitted he had just lost his head. "You know," he said with perfect sincerity, "if a coconut fell on me now, I wouldn't make a sound."

And from then on, the Dog and the easygoing Turtle were even more affectionate friends.

One fine day not long after, they decided to try again for some of the coconuts. Early the next morning the Dog appeared at the Turtle's home, and once more they started on the journey to the coconut grove.

When they reached the grove, all was quiet. Many fine coconuts lay on the ground. The two friends quickly filled their bags.

Suddenly they heard a rustle in the branches. A big coconut fell —PLUNK—right on the Dog's head. The Dog forgot all his promises. He tucked his tail between his legs and ran away howling.

When he stopped running, at a safe distance from the grove, his conscience began to torment him. How could he be so cowardly? How could he be so thoughtless? The Turtle would surely fall into the Leopard's clutches. Could he rescue his friend? He felt so bad about what he had done, he decided to seek some advice.

In the forest lived a very old and very wise Snake. The Dog went to the Snake's cottage and, even though he was ashamed, told him everything. The old Snake thought and thought. Then he gave the Dog his advice.

"Go to the seashore," he said, "and gather many large shells and stones. String them on a liana fiber and put the liana around your neck. Whenever you move, it will make loud sounds. Then go to the river and wait. When the Leopard comes to the river, make as big a racket and clatter with the shells and stones as you can. The Leopard will think the noise comes from some horrible monster hiding in the water, and he will run away. Even the Lion will not be brave enough to come near the river. This will save your friend."

The Dog was delighted with such sage advice, even though he did not quite understand how the Snake's scheme would work. Barking with joy, he ran down to the seashore as fast as he could and began to gather stones and shells.

As the Dog feared, the Leopard had captured the Turtle. To be sure, the Turtle tried to escape, but in vain. This time the Leopard had brought along his own bag.

Once again the animals gathered at the Leopard's house, ready for a fine feast. But just as the last guest arrived, the Leopard's wife discovered that there was no water in the house. The Leopard sent his children to the river to get some. While the guests waited, he tried to entertain them by telling how he caught the Turtle under a palm tree. The poor Turtle passed in turn from the Lion's claws to the Hyena's paws.

All of a sudden, a terrible howling and crying was heard outside.

The little leopards, pale with fear, had returned from the river. They could hardly tell the story of the awful monster that had tried to attack them.

When the Hyena heard this, he scoffed. "Stupid little kittens, I didn't know you were so cowardly." And he went down to the river himself. Soon he returned, with his hair standing on end. He was so terrified he couldn't speak.

Then the Gorilla went, but soon he came back, roaring and trembling all over.

The Lion spoke. "I will have to go to the river myself," he said, "to see if you are all cowards."

In a very short time he was back, his mane erect and terror in his eyes. "I have lived many years," he whispered hoarsely, "but I never heard such a monster."

The animals were seized with fright. "What can we do?" they asked each other.

Slowly the Elephant lumbered to his feet. "I am not afraid," he said. "I will go to the river, and I will return with water in my trunk!"

The other animals waited for him, fear in their hearts. No one spoke a word.

Soon the Elephant reappeared. In a breaking voice he told of the terrifying noise he had heard. He was so frightened he could not even lower his trunk into the river.

The animals trembled and shook. They looked at the Leopard. As he had threatened to tear to pieces anyone who took a coconut, he was obviously the one to fight the monster.

But the Leopard was as cowardly as he was selfish. He did not dare go down to the river alone. "My dear friends," he said quickly, "I have a plan. If we hope to catch and destroy this monster, we must join forces."

There was a great stir among the animals. Some liked the Leopard's plan. Others, more fainthearted, wanted no part of it. Finally, however, all of them went to the river, with the Lion in the lead followed by the Leopard and the Elephant and all the others.

When the last frightened animal had left, the Turtle, forgotten by everybody, crept quietly out the door and hastened to get as far as he could from the Leopard's house.

When he was well out in the bush, he heard cheerful barking. It was his friend the Dog who raced to his side, jumping and wagging his tail.

"I fooled them!" the Dog cried. "I was the monster!"

The Turtle stared at his friend in amazement.

"You should see them now," chortled the Dog. "They are standing by the river shivering with fear. The Leopard is pushing the Lion, the Elephant is pushing the Leopard, the Gorilla is pushing the Elephant and the Hyena is pushing the Gorilla."

"My dear friend," said the Turtle, "I thought you had deserted me. Instead you have saved my life. I was so sure my time had come. How can I ever repay you?"

"Oh, it was nothing," said the Dog modestly, lowering his eyes. "Anything for a friend."

And off they went, hand in hand.

Famous Female Authors

STEPHENIE MEYER

Author of the TWILIGHT SERIES

by Lori Mortensen

Snap Books are published by Capstone Press,
1710 Roe Crest Drive, North Mankato, Minnesota 56003
www.mycapstone.com

Cataloging-in-Publication Data is on file with the Library of Congress.
ISBN 978-1-5157-1329-6 (library binding)
ISBN 978-1-5157-1337-1 (paperback)
ISBN 978-1-5157-1341-8 (eBook PDF)

Editorial Credits
Abby Colich, editor; Bobbi Wyss designer;
Kelly Garvin, media researcher; Laura Manthe, production specialist

Photo Credits
Alamy: Ben Molyneux, 21, The Protected Art Archive, 5; AP: Matt Sayles, 25, Todd Williamson/Invision for Sony, 29; Corbis/Steven Georges/Press-Telegram, 19; Getty Images: George Frey, 10; Newscom: David Edwards Image Collection, 28, DVS iPhoto Inc., 6, Michael Melia/Retna/Photoshot, 26, Richie Buxo/Splash News, 15; Shutterstock: 89 studio, 9 (bottom), 17 (b), 27, Andrey Bayda, 17 (top), dugdax, 4, jaguar PS, 22, jessicakirsh, 9 (t), Netfalls-Remy Musser, cover, 1, Ollyy, 11, Undrey, 13

Printed in China.
007736

TABLE OF CONTENTS

CHAPTER 1

A Dream Come True

Stephenie Meyer had an unusual dream the night of June 2, 2003. In a sunlit meadow surrounded by a dark forest, a boy and a girl were talking. It was a strange sight. The boy was a beautiful vampire. His skin sparkled in the sun like diamonds. The girl was an ordinary human. They were deeply in love, except there was a teensy problem ...

He was dying to kill her!

It's a vampire thing.

The impossible love story captured Stephenie's imagination. It was a romance doomed to fail, right?

✔ FACT

One of the most famous novels about vampires is *Dracula*. Bram Stoker **published** this story in 1897. The book is so popular that it has never gone **out of print**. Stephenie had never read this book before writing *Twilight*.

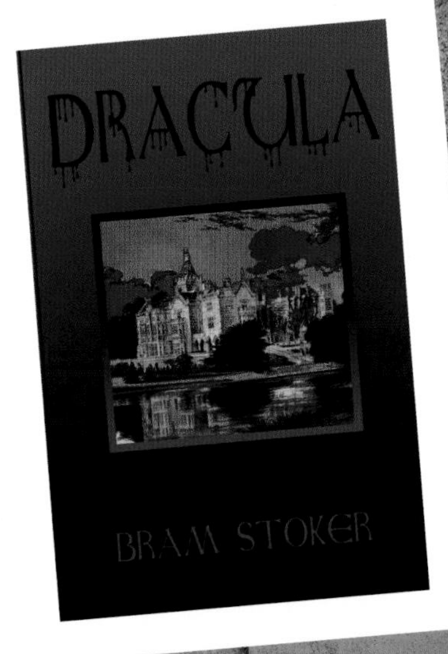

publish—to produce and distribute a book, magazine, newspaper, or any other printed material so that people can buy it

out of print—when new copies of a book title are no longer being printed

VAMPIRE DREAMING

Stephenie wondered why she was dreaming about vampires. She hadn't recently watched any vampire movies. She wasn't reading any books about vampires. This dream seemed to come out of nowhere.

Stephenie woke around 4:00 a.m. She lay in bed trying to remember each detail of the dream before it faded away. But soon enough this stay-at-home mother had to get out of bed. She had a busy day ahead taking care of her three young sons.

WRITING IT ALL DOWN

When Stephenie finally found a moment of free time later in the day, she rushed to her computer. "In the sunlight, he was shocking ..." she began typing.

One page. Two pages. By the end of the day, she had written 10 pages. These pages eventually became Chapter 13 of her first book, *Twilight*. Stephenie didn't set out to write a book. She only wanted to capture the scene from her dream. But when she finished, she couldn't stop wondering what would happen next.

Stephenie Meyer

FROM FIRST BOOK TO BEST SELLER

Three months later Stephenie had finished a 500-page book. It was an amazing feat. She had never written a book of any size before. But it was just a lark, written only for herself. And she was OK with that. No one else would want to read it anyway, she thought.

Stephenie was wrong—big time!

Soon after its 2005 release, sales launched *Twilight* to number 1 on *The New York Times* Best Sellers list. Its **sequels** *New Moon*, *Eclipse*, and *Breaking Dawn* became staples on the list for several years. Later the books became blockbuster movies, earning billions of dollars at the box office.

Stephenie Meyer—an ordinary mom with a dream—became a literary superstar.

> "Once I'd written everything that I'd dreamed, I was eager to know more about what would happen to these intriguing characters. So I kept typing, letting the story go where it wanted to go."
>
> —Stephenie Meyer interview with Cynsations blog, March 27, 2006

sequel—a story that carries the existing one forward

CHAPTER 2

Passion for Classics

Stephenie Morgan was born on Christmas Eve in Hartford, Connecticut, in 1973. Her parents named her after her father, Stephen, by adding an "ie" to the end of his name. When she was 4, her family moved to Phoenix, Arizona.

Stephenie came from a large family. She often helped take care of her younger siblings. When she wasn't busy being a big sister, she read books—lots of them. By age 8 she was reading novels written for adults. *Gone with the Wind* and *Pride and Prejudice* were on her reading list. Young Stephenie read all types of books—except horror. She was too chicken.

HIGH SCHOOL YEARS

Stephenie was a first-rate student in high school, but she felt like an outsider. There were fancy cars in the student parking lot. Some girls had plastic surgery to enhance their looks. Stephenie didn't put too much thought into her looks. She didn't even have a car.

Stephenie worked hard, and it paid off. She won the **National Merit Scholarship**. She graduated from high school in 1992.

National Merit Scholarship—a special award that comes with money for college given to the top high school students in the country

WHAT'S IN A NAME?

Stephenie chose the names of her main characters in *Twilight* carefully. She named the vampire Edward for the Edwards in two of her favorite books—*Jane Eyre* by Charlotte Brontë and *Sense and Sensibility* by Jane Austen. Stephenie's female character felt as dear to her as her own child. So Stephenie gave her the name she had been saving for if she ever had a daughter, Isabella.

MORE READER THAN WRITER

After high school, Stephenie attended Brigham Young University in Provo, Utah. She majored in English. Stephenie's love for reading led her to focus on literature.

Although Stephenie loved to read, writing was different. "I was terrified of creative writing," said Stephenie. "I did not think the stories I told myself would be interesting to anyone else, and I did not know if I could produce on command."

Stephenie took one writing class in college only because she had to. She chose poetry. She thought she could bluff her way through it.

Stephenie received her degree in English from Brigham Young University in 1997.

A LIFE OF READING

When she was 21, Stephenie married Christian Meyer. He was a friend she had known since childhood. Three years later she graduated from college. Eventually she became the mother to three boys—Gabe, Eli, and Seth. Stephenie spent some of her free time scrapbooking. She made fancy Halloween costumes for her sons. But reading was her true passion. While she cradled a baby in one arm, she held a book in the other. Stephenie often read five or six novels a week.

She had no idea that one night a whole new story would start with one dream.

FACT

Vampire characteristics vary in different stories. The traditional definition of a vampire is "a corpse that rises at night to drink the blood of the living." Often vampires are portrayed with long fangs and a black cape. Stephenie invented her own kind of vampire for *Twilight*.

CHAPTER 3

Dreaming Big

At first Stephenie did not tell anyone she was writing a book about vampires. She thought others would think it sounded cheesy. So without explanation, she dropped out of sight and wrote. No scrapbooking. No going to the movies. No long talks with friends.

But she could not disappear forever. When Stephenie stopped returning phone calls and e-mails, her sister Emily wanted to know why. Stephenie finally spilled the beans. She let her sister read what she had been writing. Emily loved it! As soon as she finished one chapter, Emily would demand to read the next. When Stephenie finally finished writing, Emily urged her to get the book published.

Publishing Fears

Stephenie didn't know anything about publishing a book. She began doing online research to learn about the process. Stephenie found everything very overwhelming.

Submitting something she'd worked so hard on was scary. It felt like turning her baby over to a stranger. What if they rejected it? Stephenie almost called it quits.

> The whole set up ... was extremely intimidating, and I almost quit there. It certainly wasn't belief in my fabulous talent that made me push forward; I think it was just that I loved my characters so much, and they were so real to me, that I wanted other people to know them, too.
>
> —Stephenie Meyer blog entry, October 5, 2005

STARTING THE PROCESS

Stephenie sent about 15 **queries** to small **literary agencies** and **publishing houses**. Several sent her rejections. Some didn't answer at all. Stephenie's younger sister Heidi told her about Janet Evanovich's website. Janet Evanovich is the successful author of several novels. On her website Janet calls the literary agency Writers House "the real thing." So Stephenie included Writers House when sending out queries. She thought such a major agency would be the least likely to respond.

Stephenie was wrong. An assistant at Writers House asked to see the first three chapters of her book. Stephenie was nervous. She didn't think that the first three chapters were the story's strongest part. A few weeks later, however, the assistant asked to see the entire manuscript. And a month after that, Stephenie got a phone call. An **agent** at Writers House wanted to represent her book!

query—a letter sent asking for information or a response
literary agency—a business that acts on behalf of writers
publishing house—a company that publishes books and magazines
agent—someone who helps a writer find a publisher

Janet Evanovich has written more than 60 romance and mystery novels for adults.

✔ FACT

Stephenie originally called her book *Forks*. This is the name of the town where the story takes place. She and her agent changed it to *Twilight* before submitting the manuscript to publishers.

CLOSING THE DEAL

Before they submitted it to publishers, Stephenie and her agent revised and polished the manuscript. Soon nine editors were interested. Little, Brown and Company, a major publisher in New York, expressed the most interest. They offered an **advance** of $300,000 for Stephenie's manuscript and two sequels. It was a staggering offer. New authors usually only receive a few thousand dollars as an advance. Publishers don't want to spend a lot of money on a book before they're sure it will sell well. This offer showed that Little, Brown thought *Twilight* would be big.

To Stephenie's horror, her agent turned down the offer. Stephenie nearly threw up.

Instead, the agent asked for a $1 million advance.

Little, Brown made a **counteroffer** of $750,000. It was the most money they had ever offered to a first-time author.

advance—a payment given prior to work being completed
counteroffer—an offer made in response to an initial offer

Hachette Book Group is located on Avenue of the Americas in New York City.

BIG CITY PUBLISHING

Most of the largest book publishing companies in the United States are located in New York City. Many authors aspire to be published by one of the "Big Five"–Hachette Book Group, HarperCollins, Macmillan, Penguin Random House, and Simon & Schuster. Stephenie's publisher, Little, Brown, is part of Hachette.

CHAPTER 4

Publishing Success

Little, Brown released *Twilight* in 2005. "It was the combination of desire and danger that drew me in," recalled Megan Tingley, the Little, Brown editor who accepted the manuscript. "On a gut level I knew I had a best seller on my hands when I was halfway through the manuscript."

Tingley was right.

In addition to reaching number 1 on *The New York Times* Best Sellers list, the magazine *Publishers Weekly* named *Twilight* one of the best children's books of 2005. The book remained a top seller for years. It was 2008's biggest selling title.

> "I was incredibly ... lucky with the publishing process. I wrote *Twilight* over the summer of 2003. I didn't think about publishing at all until it was entirely done—I was just telling myself a story. Writing just for the sake of writing, just for my own pleasure, was certainly the greatest highlight of the whole experience."
>
> —Stephenie Meyer interview with Cynsations blog, March 27, 2006

The Twilight series has sold more than 120 million copies worldwide and was translated into 38 languages.

WRITING THE SEQUELS

Stephenie had written *Twilight* with ease. Thinking that no one would ever read her story, she didn't put any pressure on herself to write something great. Writing the sequels was different. Now millions of eyes were waiting to pounce on every word. Stephenie found this challenging. Eventually, though, she got into a new groove. She wrote three more titles for the series.

In 2006 Little, Brown released *New Moon*, the second book in the series. It spent more than 25 weeks at number 1 on *The New York Times* Best Sellers list. The novel became a global **phenomenon**. Fans celebrated with midnight parties and vampire-themed proms. During the next two years, Stephenie finished *Eclipse* and *Breaking Dawn*. *Breaking Dawn* broke records by selling 1.3 million copies in the United States in the first 24 hours.

✔ FACT

Stephenie writes to music. Her favorite artists include Muse, Linkin Park, My Chemical Romance, Coldplay, The All American Rejects, Travis, Brand New, U2, Jimmy Eat World, and Weezer.

phenomenon—a very unusual or remarkable event

BOOK LEAK

In 2008 Stephenie began writing a new book, *Midnight Sun*. Then 12 chapters of the rough draft were leaked on the Internet. The novel was to be *Twilight* retold from Edward's perspective. After the leak Stephenie decided to stop working on the novel indefinitely. She thought that the unauthorized release of the manuscript would influence her writing too much.

Robert Pattinson and Kristen Stewart starred in the movie versions of the Twilight books.

HITTING HOLLYWOOD

In 2008 *Twilight* hit the big screen. Stephenie was thrilled with the cast. She was able to make suggestions during production. One change she requested was to tone down a kissing scene between Edward and Bella. Stephenie thought it was too much too soon. Their relationship needed to deepen over time. The director agreed. He reshot the scene.

Although Stephenie was involved with the production, she had no idea how the final product would turn out. When it was time to see a **rough cut**, Stephenie was terrified. If the movie was horrible, she would be heartbroken. Stephenie came prepared to make a list of everything she wanted to change. By the end, however, she had not written a word. It was everything she had hoped it would be.

The remaining movies in the Twilight saga—*New Moon, Eclipse, Breaking Dawn Part 1,* and *Breaking Dawn Part 2*—hit theaters over the next four years. All five films grossed billions of dollars worldwide, cementing the franchise's place in history.

✔ FACT

Stephenie has a **cameo** in the *Twilight* movie. At a restaurant before the camera focuses on Bella and her father, a waitress serves a veggie plate to a woman at the counter. That woman is Stephenie!

rough cut—an edited, yet not final, version of a film
cameo—a brief appearance by a celebrity

CHAPTER 5

Twilight and Beyond

Since *Twilight*'s phenomenal success, a lot has changed. Stephenie has made appearances around the world. She has talked with thousands of fans and signed countless autographs. She enjoys meeting her fans. Stephenie says that if you are not writing for teenage girls, you are missing a lot of love.

But not everything has changed. Stephenie has not let the hoopla surrounding her books go to her head. She prefers to be at home rather than anywhere else.

Stephenie continues to write, balancing her time with her family. "I mostly write at night, from eight—when my kids go to bed—till whenever I am close to passing out from exhaustion," said Stephenie. "I edit sometimes during the day, but the words never really flow the same when I am being constantly interrupted."

> "I think that after 30 years of being the most normal person in the whole world, it's really hard to become ungrounded. When I'm not out on tour or doing photo shoots, I tend to just forget about it all."
>
> —Stephenie Meyer interview with *USA Today*, July 30, 2008

Stephenie takes a selfie with a fan at the Eclipse *movie premier.*

OTHER WRITING

Before the release of *Breaking Dawn*, Stephenie published a novel for adults. *The Host* is a **paranormal** romance between a body-snatching alien and her boyfriend. Stephenie got the idea during a long drive between Phoenix and Salt Lake City. To fill the time, she told herself a story. It wasn't long before she knew she'd latched onto another winning story line. With the success of the Twilight series behind her, *The Host* debuted at number 1 on *The New York Times* Best Sellers list. Stephenie was thrilled to prove she wasn't "just a vampire girl."

The Host ***became a film in 2013.***

A BOOK FOR CHARITY

In 2010 Stephenie released *The Short Second Life of Bree Tanner.* This **novella** tells the story of Bree, whom readers first met as a newborn vampire in *Eclipse*. Stephenie donated $1.5 million of proceeds from the book to the American Red Cross. "It's amazing to have the opportunity to help those so greatly in need," Stephenie said.

paranormal—a genre of writing that deals with topics that can't be explained by science
novella—a work of fiction longer than a short story but shorter than a novel

WRITING PROCESS

Stephenie has an unusual writing process. She starts with the most exciting scenes first. Then she builds more scenes from those. When each section is finished, she finds ways to tie them together. She likes this process. As she stitches scenes together, it picks up speed like a train zooming down the tracks until it reaches its final destination—the end of the story.

Stephenie at a book signing for Life and Death

Future Projects

In 2013 Stephenie produced the movie *Austenland*. It is a romantic comedy that reconnected her with beloved classic Jane Austen literature.

Stephenie announced another new novel in 2015 for the 10th anniversary of *Twilight*. *Life and Death: Twilight Reimagined* is the *Twilight* story retold with the male and females roles reversed. Beau is a teenage boy in love with a vampire girl named Edythe.

No doubt, Stephenie has many new projects on the horizon. But whether they are sparked by a dream, a long stretch of road, or her love of classic literature, Stephenie is not just waiting around. She does not have the time. She's too busy living her dream.

Stephenie with the director and writer of Austenland

Glossary

advance (ad-VANSS)—a payment given prior to work being completed

agent (AY-juhnt)—someone who helps a writer find a publisher

cameo (KA-me-yoh)—a brief appearance by a celebrity

counteroffer (KAUN-tuhr-OFF-uhr)—an offer made in response to an initial offer

literary agency (LIT-uhr-air-ee AY-juhn-see)—a business that acts on behalf of writers

National Merit Scholarship (NASH-uh-nuhl mare-ET SKOL-ur-ship)—a special award that comes with money for college given to the top high school students in the country

novella (NO-vehl-uh)—a work of fiction longer than a short story but shorter than a novel

out of print (OUT OF PRINT)—when new copies of a book title are no longer being printed

paranormal (pair-uh-NOR-muhl)—a genre of writing that deals with topics that can't be explained by science

phenomenon (fe-NOM-uh-non)—a very unusual or remarkable event

publish (PUHB-lish)—to produce and distribute a book, magazine, newspaper, or any other printed material so that people can buy it

publishing house (PUHB-lish-eeng HOWSE)—a company that publishes books and magazines

query (KWARE-ee)—a letter sent asking for information or a response

rough cut (RUHF CUT)—an edited, yet not final, version of a film

sequel (SEE-kwel)—a story that carries the existing one forward

Read More

Guillain, Charlotte. *What Is a Novel?* Connect with Text. Chicago: Heinemann Raintree, 2015.

Owen, Ruth. *Vampires and Other Bloodsuckers.* Not Near Normal: The Paranormal. New York: Bearport Publishing, 2013.

Scherer, Lauri S. *Stephenie Meyer.* People in the News. Detroit: Lucent Books, 2012.

Internet Sites

FactHound offers a safe, fun way to find Internet sites related to this book. All of the sites on FactHound have been researched by our staff.

Here's all you do:

Visit *www.facthound.com*

Type in this code: 9781515713296

www.FACTHOUND.com®

Check out projects, games and lots more at **www.capstonekids.com**

Critical Thinking Using the Common Core

1. Where did Stephenie Meyer get the idea for the Twilight series? (Key Idea and Details)
2. What if Stephenie's sister had not pushed her to get *Twilight* published? Do you think she ever would have tried to get her book published? Explain why or why not. (Integration of Knowledge and Ideas)
3. Reread the text on page 24 and look at the photo on page 25. What feelings do you think Stephenie had while this photo was being taken? (Craft and Structure)

Index